Thank you to the generous team wh.... g....
and talents to make this book possible.

Writer
Lizzie Iwicki

Creative Directors
Caroline Kurtz and Jane Kurtz

Artists
Lizzie Iwicki
Children from Christa McAuliffe Elementary School
Children from Ethiopian Community Center of Seattle

Designer
Sarah Richards

Translator
Amlaku B. Eshetie

Ready Set Go Books, an Open Hearts Big Dreams Project

Special thanks to Ethiopia Reads donors and staff for
believing in this project and helping get it started-- and for
arranging printing, distribution, and training in Ethiopia.

10/30/18

The Happiest Herder in the Land

በምድሪቷ ላይ ደስተኛው እረኛ

Long ago, a goat herder named Kaldi lived in Ethiopia.

ዱሮ ዱሮ ካልዲ የሚባል ኢትዮጵያዊ የፍየል እረኛ ኢትዮጵያ ውስጥ ነበር።

Every day, Kaldi watched over his goats as they grazed.

ካልዲ በየዕለቱ ፍየሎቹን ቅጠሎችን በብዛት
ሊያገኙበት ወደሚችሉበት ደን ያስማራቸዋል።

He played his flute for the goats.

ከዚያም ለፍየሎቹ ዋሽንቱን ይነፋላቸው ነበር።

They always listened quietly to his music.

እነሱም ቅጠሎቻቸን እየተመገቡ ዋሽንቱን ያዳምጡ ነበር።

But one day, Kaldi could not find his goats.

ከዕለታት አንድ ቀን ግን ፍየሎቹ ጠፉበት።

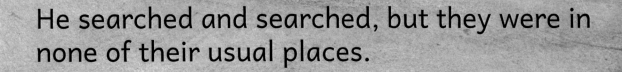

He searched and searched, but they were in
none of their usual places.

ፈለገ፤ ፈለገ፤ ግን ሁልጊዜ ሊሰማሩባቸው
በሚችሉ በየትኛውም ቦታ አልነበሩም።

Finally, he stumbled upon
his goats in the woods,
where he saw them leaping
and dancing and playing.

በመጨረሻም፣ በጫካው ውስጥ አንድ አካባቢ
እየዘለሉና እየፈነጩ ድንገት አገኛቸው።

Kaldi was scared.

ካልዲ ፈርቶ ነበር።

He hid and watched, wondering what had made the goats so happy.

ፍየሎቹን ምን እንደሚያዘልላቸውና እንደሚያስፈነጫቸው ስላላወቀ ተደብቆ ይመለከታቸው ነበር፡፡

Then he saw the goats eating red berries.

ከዚያም ፍየሎቹ ቀያይና ትናንሽ ፍሬዎችን
ከአንድ ዛፍ ላይ ሲበሉ አያቸው።

His goats leaped and danced and played until it was evening.

ፍየሎቹም እስከማታ ድረስ
እየዘለሉና እየፈነጩ ነበር።

Even as night fell, they did not want to sleep.

መሽቶም እንኳ ወደ ጋጣቸው መግባትና መተኛት አልፈለጉም ነበር።

Kaldi decided he had to try some of those berries. Soon, he felt very happy!

ካልዲ ከነዚያ ፍሬዎች ጥቂቶቹን ለመቅመስና ለመሞከር ወሰነ። እንደቀመሰውም ደስ የሚል ስሜት ተሰማው።

He joined his dancing goats.

የሚዘሉትና የሚፈነጭትን ፍየሎች ተቀላቀላቸው፡፡

Kaldi became the happiest herder in the land.

ካልዲ በምድሪቲ ውስጥ በጣም ደስተኛው እረኛ ሆነ።

And that is an old, old story of how coffee beans were discovered in Ethiopia.

ይህም ቡና ለመጀመሪያ ጊዜ በኢትዮጵያ ውስጥ እንዴት እንደተገኘ የሚያስረዳ የዱሮ ጊዜ ታሪክ ነው::

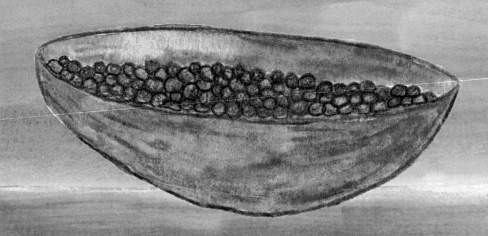

Behind the Story

Lizzie Iwicki was thrilled to have the opportunity to create a Ready Set Go Book. As the goal of the project is to create children's books inspired by Ethiopian stories, myths, or proverbs, she began her search on the internet by reading many Ethiopian folktales. She came across the legend of how coffee was discovered in Ethiopia, a fact not many people know, between 900 and 1000 A.D. when the country was often called Abyssinia. Coffee is a very popular drink in her home state of Washington, where there is a coffee shop on every corner. She thought this would be a fun book for Ready Set Go Books because the images of the goats leaping would be joyful for the readers. She hopes that readers in Ethiopia will enjoy her book and that they will learn something interesting about their country's history.

About Open Hearts Big Dreams

Open Hearts Big Dreams began as a volunteer organization, led by **Ellenore Angelidis** in Seattle, Washington, to provide sustainable funding and strategic support to Ethiopia reads, collaborating with **Jane Kurtz**. OHBD has now grown to be its own nonprofit organization supporting literacy, art, and technology for young people in Ethiopia.

Ellenore comes from a family of teachers who believe education is a human right, and opportunity should not depend on your birthplace. And as the adoptive mother of a little girl who was born in Ethiopia and learned to read in the U.S., as well as an aspiring author, she finds the chance to positively impact literacy hugely compelling!

About the Author

Lizzie Iwicki is a high school senior at Eastside Catholic High School in Sammamish, WA. Besides her studies, Lizzie is a soccer team captain, a member of theNa tional Honor Society, and a Girl Up Club member. She is currently in the process of determining where she would like to attend college. While in college, she also plans to play collegiate soccer and hopes to study abroad.

Lizzie has volunteered with Open Hearts Big Dreams for the last four years and this past year became a Junior Board member. She has always enjoyed working with children whether volunteering in the classroom at her local elementary school, being a summer camp counselor, or helping with the children's liturgy at her parish. She has always loved reading and has special memories of some of her favorite childhood books filled with entertaining stories and colorful pictures.

About the Illustrators

After writing the story, **Lizzie** wanted to involve children in the artwork for the book. She led an art session with her fourth grade teacher **Ms. Toth's class at Christa McAuliffe Elementary School,** where the students worked on a variety of pictures. She also used a few background scenes painted by the children at the **Ethiopian Community Center of Seattle**. Besides having fun working on the art, the children were all very excited about the mission of Ready Set Go Books. To complete the project, Lizzie created the remaining art, including the main character Kaldi, the goats, and some of the backgrounds. She also developed the layout for the book by combining the watercolor scenes with the pencil drawn characters to create colorful and lively pages for the readers to enjoy.

About Ready Set Go Books

Reading has the power to change lives, but many children and adults in Ethiopia cannot read. One reason is that Ethiopia has very few books in local languages to give people a chance to practice reading. Ready Set Go books wants to close that gap and open a world of ideas and possibibilities for kids and their communities.

When you buy a Ready Set Go book, you provide critical funding to create and distribute more books.

Learn more at: http://openheartsbigdreams.org/book-project/

Ready Set Go 10 Books

In 2018, Ready Set Go Books decided to experiment by trying a few new books in larger sizes.

Sometimes it was the art that needed a little more room to really shine. Sometimes the story or nonfiction text was a bit more complicated than the short and simple text used in most of our current early reader books.

We are calling these our "Ready Set Go 10" books as a way to show these ones are bigger and also sometimes have more words on the page. We are happy to hear feedback on these new books and on all our books.

About the Language

Amharic is a Semetic language -- in fact, the world's second-most widely spoken Semetic language, after Arabic. Starting in the 12th century, it became the Ethiopian language that was used in official transactions and schools and became widely spoken all over Ethiopia. It's written with its own characters, over 260 of them. Eritrea and Ethiopia share this alphabet, and they are the only countries in Africa to develop a writing system centuries ago that is still in use today!

About the Translation

Translation is currently being coordinated by a volunteer, **Amlaku Bikss Eshetie** who has a BA degree in Foreign Languages & Literature, an MA in Teaching English as a Foreign Language, and PhD courses in Applied Linguistics and Communication, all at Addis Ababa University. He taught English from elementary through university levels and is currently a passionate and experienced English-Amharic translator. As a father of three, he also has a special interest in child literacy and development. He can be reached at: khaabba_ils@protonmail.com

Find more Ready Set Go Books on Amazon.com

To view all available titles, search "Ready Set Go Ethiopia" or scan QR code

 Chaos

 Talk Talk Turtle

 The Glory of Gondar

 We Can Stop the Lion

 Not Ready!

 Fifty Lemons

 Count For Me

 Too Brave

 Tell Me What You Hear

93700140R00020

Made in the USA
San Bernardino, CA
09 November 2018